LaRue for Mayor

Letters from the Campaign Trail

Written and Illustrated by
Mark Teague

The Blue Sky Press An Imprint of Scholastic Inc. New York

The Snort City Regis

September 30

THE BLUE SKY PRESS

For Butch

Library of Congress Cataloging-in-Publication Data available.

ISBN-13: 978-0-439-78315-6
ISBN-10: 0-439-78315-1

Printed in Singapore 46

First printing, March 2008
Designed by David Saylor and Lillie Mear

BUGWORT LAUNCHES CAMPAIGN FOR MAYOR

Former Pumpkinville police chief Hugo Bugwort announced yesterday that he will run for mayor of Snort City. Calling himself the "Law and Order" candidate, Bugwort, who spoke to a cheering crowd in Gruber Park, is widely considered a shoo-in for the job. "Snort City is a disgrace!" he said, to polite applause. "We need to be more like Pumpkinville. That means no more sloppiness, no more silliness, and no more foolish behavior." The speech was interrupted when several dogs in the back of the crowd overturned a hot-dog cart. Injured in the fracas was Gertrude LaRue of Second Avenue. The dogs were not identified.

DOGS DISRUPT RALLY

October 1

Dear Mrs. LaRue,

How sorry I am to hear about your injuries! Who knew that hot-dog carts were so unstable? I was simply trying to get a better view of Chief Bugwort when it collapsed. Heaven knows what those other dogs were doing. I must admit that they created an unfortunate impression of delinquency. Anyway, I'm shocked to hear that you'll be confined to the hospital for so long.

No doubt you are worried about me. So am I! But Mrs. Hibbins has promised to serve my meals, and somehow I will persevere.

With Deepest Sympathy,
Ike

Get Well Soon

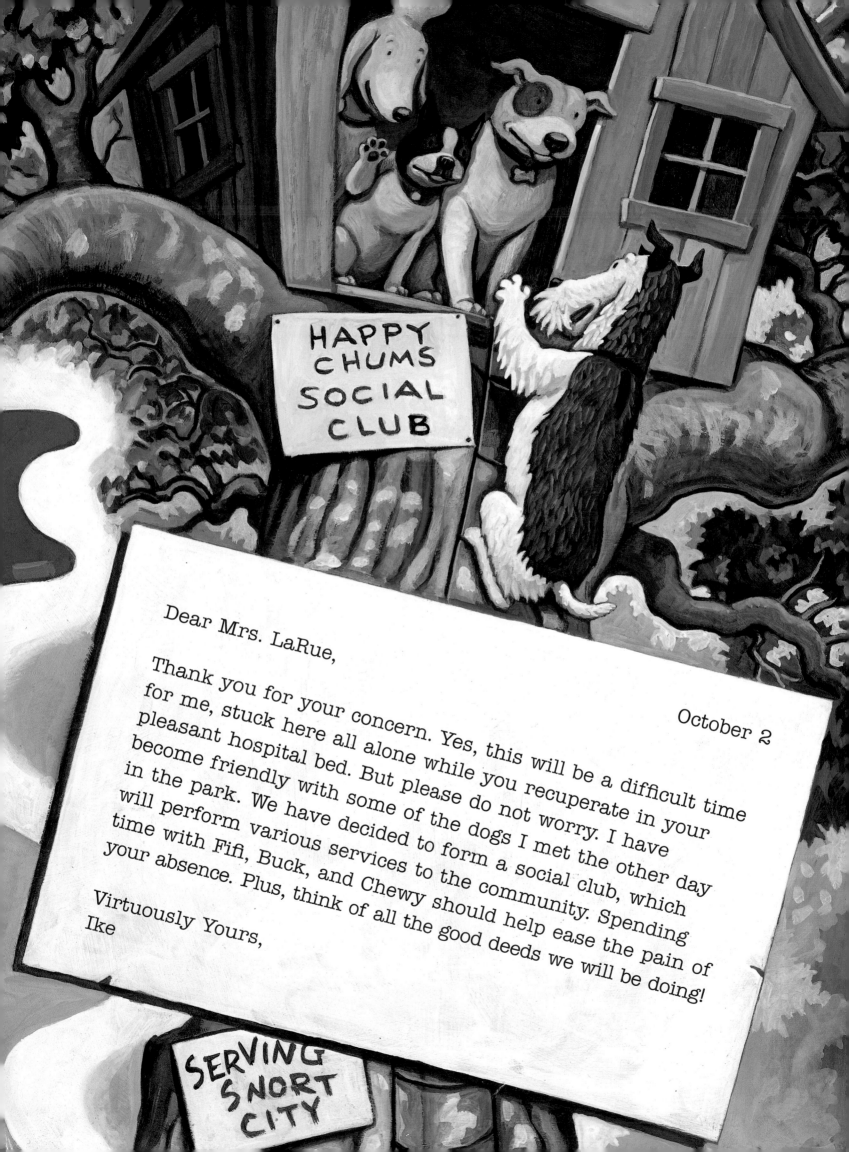

HAPPY
CHUMS
SOCIAL
CLUB

SERVING
SNORT
CITY

Dear Mrs. LaRue,

October 2

Thank you for your concern. Yes, this will be a difficult time for me, stuck here all alone while you recuperate in your pleasant hospital bed. But please do not worry. I have become friendly with some of the dogs I met the other day in the park. We have decided to form a social club, which will perform various services to the community. Spending time with Fifi, Buck, and Chewy should help ease the pain of your absence. Plus, think of all the good deeds we will be doing!

Virtuously Yours,
Ike

Wild Dogs Rampage!
Game Disrupted

Unruly dogs plagued Snort City again yesterday, as one of the animals broke up a double play and ran away with the baseball during a Snort City Rabbits game at Morley Field. The episode capped a week of problems that began on Tuesday when a pack of the rambunctious creatures broke up the annual Fishin' Derby on Blat Lake. Apparently the dogs first rolled in, then ate, the catch. The following day a group of dogs snuck into a "Mr. Ding-a-Ling" truck outside Gruber Park and made off with two gallons of rocky road ice cream. None of the dogs have been apprehended, though ice-cream vendor Eugene Phelps describes the leader as a "scruffy black-and-white fellow."

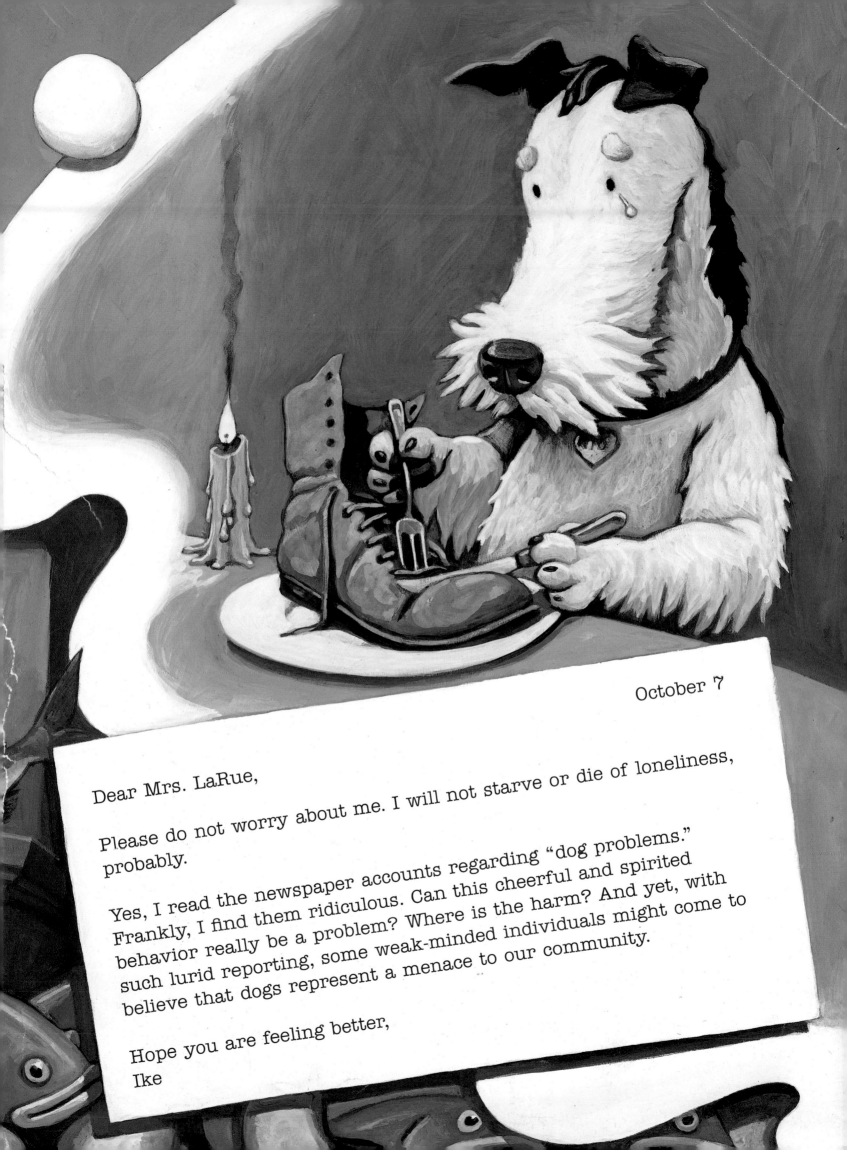

October 7

Dear Mrs. LaRue,

Please do not worry about me. I will not starve or die of loneliness, probably.

Yes, I read the newspaper accounts regarding "dog problems." Frankly, I find them ridiculous. Can this cheerful and spirited behavior really be a problem? Where is the harm? And yet, with such lurid reporting, some weak-minded individuals might come to believe that dogs represent a menace to our community.

Hope you are feeling better,
Ike

The Snort City Register/Gazette

Bugwort Calls for Canine Crackdown

Calling dogs "a menace to our community," mayoral candidate Hugo Bugwort yesterday announced his plans to crack down on the beasts. "We can no longer tolerate this sort of behavior," he said, citing recent dog-related problems. Mr. Bugwort proposes not only a leash law and a curfew, but a complete ban on the animals in most public places. "This town is literally going to the dogs," said Bugwort. "I intend to stop it."

In related news, a dog reportedly snuck into Branmeier's Butcher Shop on Second Avenue and made off with a string of beef sausages.

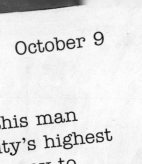

Dear Mrs. LaRue,

I must say I have become alarmed by the ravings of this man Bugwort. Imagine if he actually were elected to our city's highest office! The idea is unthinkable. I must figure out some way to stop this impending disaster!

Your Worried Dog,
Ike

The Snort City Register/Gazette

Letters to the Editor:

As a longtime resident, I must decry the wave of anti-dog hysteria sweeping over our city. Can we so quickly forget the loyalty of Man's Best Friend? Who accompanies our firefighters and police on their perilous rounds? Who rescues the weary traveler stuck high in the Alps? Who serves the blind (and the deaf, too, most likely)? Dogs, that's who!

Signed,
A Concerned Citizen

October 11

Dear Mrs. LaRue,

How I envy you the safety of your hospital bed! Here in the
outside world, things have become perilous indeed—at least
for dogs! The awful Bugwort continues his scurrilous attacks.
Yesterday he referred to dogs as "gangs of hooligans." He
must be stopped. Therefore I have decided to "throw my hat
into the ring." This afternoon I will announce my candidacy.
Doubtless the public response will be overwhelming.

Your Next Mayor,
Ike

Dear Mrs. LaRue,   October 12

My first day on the campaign trail was fabulous! Everywhere huge crowds
turned out to cheer my message of dog-friendliness. My chums from the
social club have agreed to help. Of course we will do our best to keep this
campaign positive, though I can't speak for my opponent, who appears to be
vicious and unstable, if not insane.

Honestly Yours,
Ike

October 13

Dear Mrs. LaRue,

In my appearances I have been pointing out that if dogs are banned from places like Gruber Park, cats will run wild. Not a pleasant thought! The campaign continues to gather steam. I think we have Bugwort on the ropes.

Politically Yours,
Ike

P.S. I hope you don't mind, but I have been using the apartment as campaign headquarters.

The Snort City Register/Gazette

October 14

Bugwort Challenged by Mystery Candidate!

A mysterious new candidate has emerged to challenge Hugo Bugwort in his run for mayor. Supporters of Ike LaRue describe him as "dog-friendly." Opponents point out that he is, in fact, a dog. Either way, the furry LaRue has begun to wage a fierce campaign against Bugwort, who promises to virtually ban all dogs from Snort City. Surprisingly, LaRue's message has begun to catch on. "We didn't anticipate this," admits Bugwort campaign manager, Walt Smiley, referring to the dogs. "It turns out some folks are really fond of the little devils."

"I'm not worried," said Bugwort. "Tomorrow is my big rally in Gruber Park. I'll deal with these dog-lovers then."

Dear Mrs. LaRue,

October 15

My supporters and I have decided to confront Chief Bugwort at today's rally. We will be out in force, and though we will conduct ourselves in a dignified manner, I am sure that the results will be interesting.

Hope you are well,
Ike

P.S. Nothing will distract me from this important cause.

LaRue Rescues Bugwort!

Dog Called Hero

Hugo Bugwort was rushed to Memorial Hospital yesterday after collapsing onstage during a rally in Gruber Park. Apparently he grew dizzy while trying to shout down hecklers. Among his rescuers was his opponent, local dog Ike LaRue. "When the Chief collapsed we rushed him to the nearest vehicle, a Mr. Ding-a-Ling truck," explained campaign manager, Walt Smiley. "For some reason the dog was already inside. But give him credit—he really did his best to help."

"LaRue saved me," said Bugwort. "All the way to the hospital he fed me cool, delicious rocky road ice cream. By the time I got here I was feeling much better." The rescue puts a new twist on an already unusual campaign. "I have completely changed my mind about dogs," said Bugwort. "In fact, I would be honored if Ike would serve with me as Assistant Mayor, to make sure that the interests of dogs are represented in a Bugwort administration." LaRue, who departed in the Mr. Ding-a-Ling truck, could not be reached for comment.

Dear Mrs. LaRue,

October 16

It turns out that Chief Bugwort is not such a bad fellow after all. In fact, he's swell! Anyway, politics are not for me. I would rather make friends than engage in this constant bickering. And since all I ever wanted was to make this a great city for EVERYONE, I have decided to wrap up my campaign and accept the Chief's offer to serve as Assistant Mayor.

I'm so glad that you are feeling better and will be able to attend my swearing-in ceremony.

Your loyal Dog,
Ike

The Snort City Register/Gazette

November 3

Bugwort Sworn In!
LaRue Joins Former Adversary

Promising to have the most dog-friendly administration ever, new mayor Hugo Bugwort was sworn in yesterday during a ceremony in Gruber Park. At his side was Assistant Mayor Ike LaRue, whom many credit with his success. "This is a great day for everyone in Snort City!" proclaimed Bugwort, to loud cheers from the audience. The speech was interrupted when several dogs in the back of the crowd overturned a hot-dog cart. Bugwort promised to look into the matter.

"It certainly is worrisome," he said.